# QUETZAL

## SACRED BIRD OF THE CLOUD FOREST

# QUETZAL

## SACRED BIRD OF THE CLOUD FOREST

*Dorothy Hinshaw Patent*

*Illustrated by Neil Waldman*

Morrow Junior Books
New York

## ACKNOWLEDGMENTS

Many people have generously contributed their time
and expertise in helping me write this book. I want especially
to thank Bettina Escudero, Laurie Hunter, Andreas Lenhoff
of Defensores de la Naturaleza, Guatemala, and George Powell.

Colored pencils were used for the full-color illustrations.
The text type is 12-point Palatino.

Text copyright © 1996 by Dorothy Hinshaw Patent
Illustrations copyright © 1996 by Neil Waldman

Printed in Hong Kong by South China Printing Company (1988) Ltd.

1 2 3 4 5 6 7 8 9 10

Library of Congress Cataloging-in-Publication Data
Patent, Dorothy Hinshaw.
Quetzal: sacred bird of the Cloud Forest/Dorothy Hinshaw Patent; illustrated by Neil Waldman.
p. cm.
Includes index.
Summary: Provides information about the quetzal, a beautiful bird found in Mexico and Central America, and about its significance in the lives and beliefs of ancient Mesoamerican peoples.
ISBN 0-688-12662-6 (trade)—ISBN 0-688-12663-4 (library)
1. Indians of Mexico—Folklore.   2. Indians of Central America—Folklore.   3. Quetzals—Folklore.
4. Quetzals—History—Juvenile literature.   5. Quetzalcoatl (Aztec deity)—Juvenile literature.   [1. Quetzals.
2. Indians of Mexico—History.   3. Indians of Central America—History.   4. Quetzalcoatl (Aztec deity).]
I. Waldman, Neil, ill.   II. Title.   F1219.3.F6P37 1996   398.2'0972045287—dc20   95-14402   CIP AC

*This book is dedicated to the conservationists
who devote their lives to saving the beautiful
wildlands of Mexico and Central America.*
—D.H.P.

*For Barbara LeVasseur,
caring friend and protector
of our feathered cousins.*
—N.W.

# CONTENTS

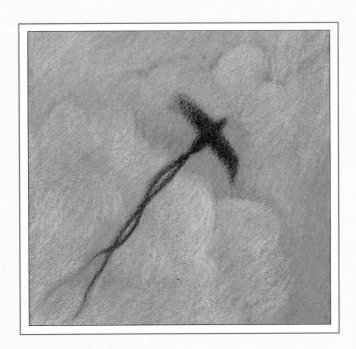

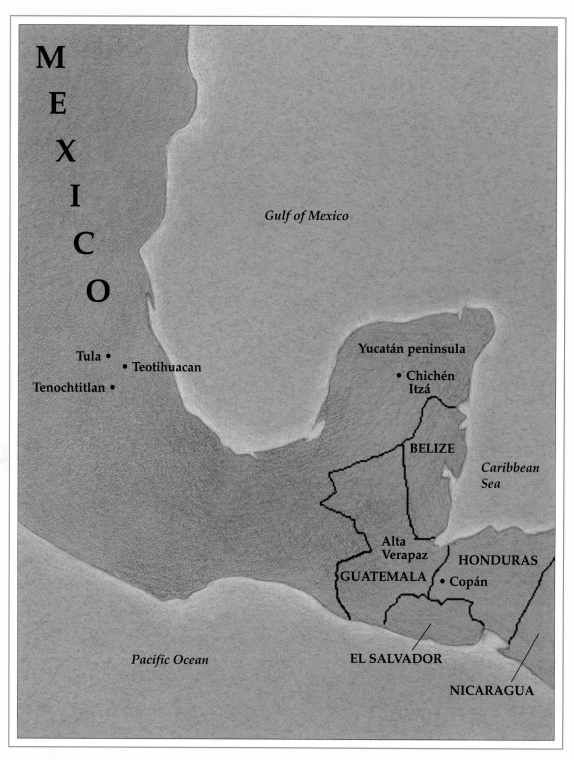

*Mesoamerica—land of the quetzal, Maya, and Aztecs.*

# INTRODUCTION

The story of the beautiful and mysterious quetzal and its relationship to people stretches further back than recorded human history. No one can know for sure the origins of stories about the bird or the sacred spirit, Quetzalcoatl, that it helped inspire, but we can make educated guesses.

The historical background of this story is very complex. It involves many different cultures, only some of which left their marks upon the historical record. Other groups, which produced no surviving monuments or relics to give clues about their ways of life, also influenced the development of human culture in Mesoamerica. In a book this size, only the best-known groups, such as the Toltecs and the Maya, can be brought into the picture. But it is important to remember that Mesoamerica has been home to a multitude of peoples whose fortunes and influences rose and fell over the ages.

Mesoamerican peoples exhibited great diversity in their spiritual lives. We actually know very little about this subject, since almost all written documents were destroyed by the conquistadores. We can only rely on the few relics that survived, on monument inscriptions, and on oral accounts written down by the Spanish shortly after the conquest. The lack of detailed information leads to another problem—disagreements among scholars about the meaning behind the archaeological record. In this book, I have tried to give the most widely accepted version of Mesoamerican history wherever there is disagreement. Time and future archaeological work could change our ideas about what really happened.

It is difficult for us to put ourselves into the lives of early Mesoamericans and see how they viewed the spiritual world. We call the individual entities to which temples were built and worship was given, such as Quetzalcoatl and Tlaloc, gods. Yet evidence suggests that the Maya and other peoples believed in a single creator with a variety of spiritual aspects that modern scholars have chosen to designate as gods. This is one reason why Catholicism was so readily adopted in the region—the Catholic saints could easily be equated with the traditional spiritual aspects of the creator in the native religions.

As you read this book, you should be aware that the information has by necessity been simplified and that there is much we will never know about the lives of both the peoples of Mesoamerica and the animals with which they shared this beautiful and varied land, such as the fabulous resplendent quetzal.

*A male quetzal flies skyward.*

# ONE

# THE FEATHERED SERPENT

THE MYSTERIOUS COOING COMES FROM trees all around, filling the dark, misty forest with sound. Then, as dawn's light begins to pale the horizon, the noise stops, and the forest is still. The sun rises quickly. Just as its rays touch the tops of the giant trees, a brilliant flash of color streaks upward into the sky, a shimmering creature that spirals as it climbs. The sunlight glints off its body—first iridescent green, then bright red and gleaming white. As it rises, the creature lets out a raucous cry: *wacka-wacka-wacka.*

The bird flies up and up until it becomes just a tiny speck against the pale blue sky. It pauses for a moment, then plunges, its body forming a straight line with its glittering green tail streamers. As it plummets into the dense forest and disappears, another takes its place, spiraling upward and calling coarsely. On and on, one after another, the gorgeous creatures snake upward into the sky, then skydive straight down to disappear into the forest.

This dramatic display takes place in remote parts of the Mexican and Central American cloud forest that crowns the mountainous backbone connecting North and South America. It is a ritual older than the earliest recorded human history, one marveled at by the first people to inhabit the Americas. The behavior of this bird—still called by its ancient name, quetzal—inspired in them a vision of unity: sky with earth, snake with bird, light with dark. The quetzal helped give rise to the image of the feathered serpent, a sacred snake cloaked in bright green feathers instead of scales, which unified these apparent opposites. This symbolic meaning has

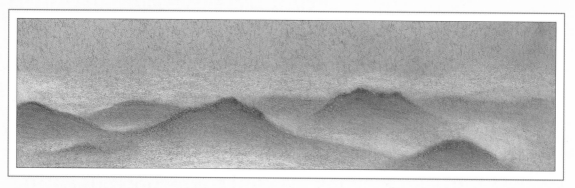

*The cloud forest, domain of the quetzal.*

lasted throughout the history of the peoples in the region called Mesoamerica, from central Mexico southward along the mountains through Central America into Nicaragua.

## THE RESPLENDENT QUETZAL

The rain forests of the Americas are home to many brilliantly colored birds—macaws, toucans, and others. Above the rain forests, the mountaintops poke up into the clouds, creating a misty realm called the cloud forest. While many plants and animals from lower elevations live here, the cloud forest is also home to species that require it for their survival. One of these is the quetzal, a unique bird that combines impressive size with brilliant iridescence. The quetzal's full name today—the resplendent quetzal—implies its glowing splendor and is a fitting name for such a beautiful bird. Scientists call it *Pharomachrus mocinno*.

The body of the quetzal is fourteen inches (36 centimeters) long and weighs just under a half pound (210 grams)—somewhat larger than a magpie. But the male's four glittering tail feathers, called coverts, can trail more than two feet (61 centimeters) behind his body. In fact, scientists have measured coverts that are almost thirty-eight inches (96 centimeters) long. The male's head is crowned by a helmet of short soft green feathers that he can puff up or slick down. His entire head, chest, upper wings, and back as well as his tail feathers shimmer an iridescent green or sometimes blue, changing with the angle of the light striking them. Sometimes the light hits him in a way that tips his helmet or body feathers with gleaming gold. His belly is bright red, and the underside of his tail, beneath the coverts, is white.

The female's body is the same size as the male's. She is more modestly colored but still very striking. Like the male, she has shimmering green feathers on her head, chest, upper wings, and back. Her belly is gray. She has a red patch under her tail, and black-and-white bars on the underside of her tail. Her tail coverts are also green, but they are much shorter than those of the male.

The resplendent quetzal belongs to a family of tropical birds called trogons. Trogons live mostly in the forest. All male trogons are colorful—with red, orange, or yellow bellies and green or purple heads and chests—but only the quetzal bears the gorgeous feathery train of metallic green that turns him into a snake bird in flight.

Through the ages, the unique beauty and stunning displays of the male quetzal have impressed the people of Mesoamerica, making the bird precious both as a symbol and as a source of one of the most valuable commodities for trade in ancient times—its feathers.

*A pair of quetzals, with the female on the left.*

*An ancient Mayan relief showing a chief wearing a quetzal-feather headdress.*

# TWO

# THE FEATHERED SERPENT'S PEOPLE

LITTLE IS KNOWN OF THE EARLY HUMAN history of Mesoamerica. No one knows when the first people arrived there, but it is certain that this key event took place thousands and thousands of years ago. Over the centuries numerous tribes developed their own ways of living on the land and explaining how the world worked. These groups traded with one another, so stories about unique creatures like the fabulous highland quetzal became familiar even to coastal peoples.

Beginning around 1200 B.C., toward the end of the Mycenaean period of Greek history, Mesoamerican cultures began to leave traces that today's archaeologists can study. In what is now Mexico, the Olmecs thrived for almost a thousand years, then vanished. The Teotihuacanos followed, then the Toltecs, and finally the Aztecs. Farther south, the Mayan civilization began its long and complex history around 1000 B.C. The early Olmecs invented a form of writing called glyph writing, and religious and cultural centers sprang up in many places from just north of present-day Mexico City south into what are now Honduras and El Salvador.

## THE MAYA

The classical Mayan culture flourished, mostly in the area now known as Guatemala, from A.D. 317 to 650. The quetzal was sacred to the Maya. Its feathers were as precious as gold. Killing a quetzal was forbidden, with death being the penalty for anyone caught. Instead, male quetzals were trapped at watering places, and their graceful plumes were plucked out before the birds were released. Since a

*A Mayan trader, with his pack propped behind him. He carries quetzal feathers, along with other items for trade.*

bird grows a new set of feathers each year, the plumes were soon replaced, and no permanent damage was done. The right to capture quetzals was inherited, and it brought great wealth to the owner.

Mayan traders supplied quetzal feathers to other Mesoamerican peoples throughout the area. Along with the feathers came stories about the fabled feathered serpent, the brilliant green snake that lived in the sky and plunged to the earth.

The Maya developed a great civilization. Their writing system was the most sophisticated anywhere in pre-Columbian America, and their mathematical system included the advanced concept of zero for the first time in the Americas. They tracked the sun, moon, Venus, and other heavenly bodies and knew their cycles in detail. They invented a complex calendar based on cycles of repeating year and day names and could project it thousands of years into either the past or the future. Their calendar was adopted by later Mesoamerican cultures. The Maya were great artists, producing many monuments, including great carved stone columns, called stelae, that portrayed spiritual entities and rulers. The stelae bore the dates on which they were produced, which has helped archaeologists anchor Mayan culture in time.

Mayan classical civilization lasted for hundreds of years. But through a series of disasters, the great Mayan centers collapsed before the year 900. The last dated classical stela was erected in A.D. 889. But the Maya weren't finished yet. Mayan peoples continued to live in the Guatemalan highlands while the center of their civilization moved mostly northward, into the lowlands of the Yucatán peninsula. There they helped develop the great city of Chichén Itzá and other centers of culture.

## CULTURES OF NORTHERN MESOAMERICA

Meanwhile, in what is now Mexico, civilization was developing through the establishment of a series of powerful city-states. The first of these was named Teotihuacan, which began as a settlement around the second century B.C. From the second century A.D. to the early eighth century A.D., Teotihuacan flourished as a great power. It was home to tens of thousands of people and contained great pyramids and temples. Paintings in brilliant green, featuring quetzal feathers and the feathered serpent, graced the walls of at least one temple in Teotihuacan. Sometime before A.D. 750, the city was destroyed by fire.

*Stone column, or stela, from the ancient Mayan center of Copán.*

17

A warlike tribe from the north, the Toltecs, filled the power void left by the destruction of Teotihuacan. Their capital was named Tula. The Toltecs dominated until Tula was destroyed by the Chichimec tribe in 1156. The Toltecs continued their culture in other cities, such as Chichén Itzá and Xicalango, which they shared with other groups, such as the Maya.

Aztec history began with the arrival of migratory tribes from the north into the valley of Mexico, south of Tula. The Aztecs settled on two small islands in Lake Texcoco, founding the city of Tenochtitlan in 1325. They developed a very successful culture based on agriculture and warfare. Over time, they formed alliances with other city-states and eventually took control over much of Mesoamerica. They created splendid works of art, including fabulous featherwork featuring quetzal plumes. They carved impressive stone images and produced colorful painted murals. But they also enslaved thousands of conquered people and sacrificed countless prisoners of war. Aztec society flourished until the disastrous arrival of the Spanish conquistador Hernando Cortés in 1519.

## AFTER THE CONQUISTADORES

By the time the Spaniards came to the New World, the magnificent cities of classical Mayan civilization had been reclaimed by the tropical forests and were known to the people only by rumor. But the Mayan people continued to live throughout much of what is now southern Mexico and down through Central America into present-day Honduras and El Salvador. The Spaniards fought their way through Central America, bringing the descendants of the proud Maya under their rule.

When the Spanish conquered the Aztecs and the descendants of the ancient Maya, they burned their sacred books, destroying valuable information on Mesoamerican history and custom. But fortunately the stones remained to help tell the tales of these societies. Statues, stelae, carvings that included writings, and a few rare books and murals—all have provided vital clues. Thanks to the dedicated people who have worked at deciphering the archaeological remains and the few Mayan and Aztec books still in existence, we now know something of the stories that inspired these accomplished cultures.

## FEATHERS FOR ADORNMENT

To this day, tribes in the deep tropical rain forests of South America produce breathtakingly beautiful masks, headdresses, clothing, and jewelry from the colorful feathers of tropical birds. In the rest of the Americas, this beautiful art has been lost.

*Staff decorated with quetzal feathers.*

No featherwork from Mayan times survives today, and only a few Aztec pieces remain of the countless works that once existed.

Fortunately we can at least learn something of how feathers were used by studying Mayan and Aztec carvings, paintings, and writings. We know that in pre-Columbian times, specialized artisans in Mesoamerica devoted their careers to making beautiful items from feathers. Even after the Mayan empire collapsed, Mayan traders carried feathers throughout Mesoamerica. The most treasured of all were those of the quetzal. Throughout Mesoamerica, only members of the ruling class and images of the gods were allowed to wear the feathers of the quetzal.

During Aztec times, especially skillful craftspeople, called the toltecah, created luxury items for the nobility. The toltecah inherited their place in society and were considered the heirs of the fine craftwork of the Toltecs. The toltecah began as apprentices and worked their way up as they learned their arts. They made jewelry from gold and precious greenstone, and they fashioned capes, shields, and fans from the most precious feathers, including those of the quetzal.

Even after Cortés conquered the Aztecs, the demand for quetzal feathers was high—in 1575, ten thousand feathers were brought to the remnant Aztec society from Alta Verapaz, where quetzals were traditionally trapped.

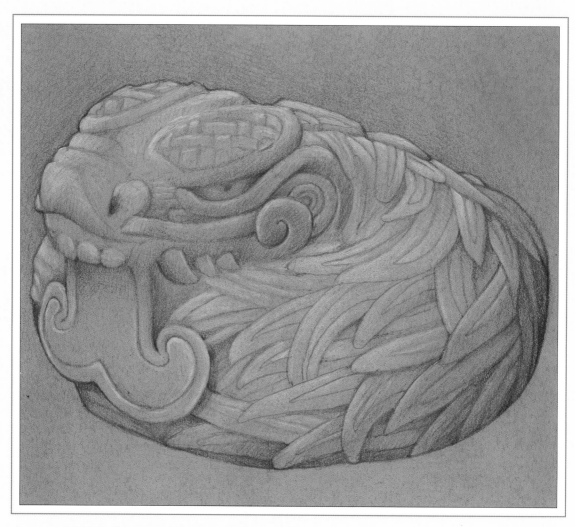

*Aztec stone image of the Plumed Serpent, Quetzalcoatl.*

# THREE

# THE FEATHERED SERPENT GOD, QUETZALCOATL

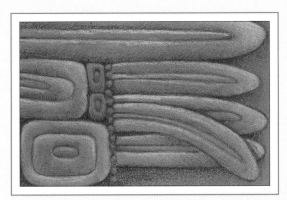

THE ANCIENT AZTEC STONE CARV-ing stares out from inside the locked case. The snakelike head, with its large, flat forked tongue, tops the coiled body overlaid with feathers. This is the Plumed Serpent, the god Quetzalcoatl, who joined with the heavenly god, Heart of Sky, to create the Earth and its living things.

## QUETZALCOATL'S BEGINNINGS

No one can be certain about the origins of Quetzalcoatl. Some experts believe this god originated as an offshoot of the jaguar cult. The Olmecs, probably the most advanced of the earliest Mesoamerican cultures, depicted an image that combined the feathered serpent with the jaguar.

However, many things about Quetzalcoatl point to his origin as a symbol associated with the mysterious quetzal instead. While the name Quetzalcoatl is usually translated as "feathered serpent" or "plumed serpent," the prefix *quetzal* refers more specifically to the resplendent quetzal itself. A Mayan name for Quetzalcoatl is Kukulcán, and to this day Mayan people in Alta Verapaz call the quetzal *kukul*. Like the resplendent quetzal, the plumed serpent is covered with bright green feathers (green was the royal color among both Maya and Aztecs). The feathered serpent, like the male quetzal spiraling upward, is associated with the sky. Even in modern times the Huichol Indians of Mexico think of rain clouds as plumed serpents.

Quetzalcoatl was also a god of the wind and had influence over the rain. The bird itself makes watchers aware of the wind, as its delicate tail feathers sway in the slightest puff of breeze. And since the spectacular displays of the male quetzal occur near the end of the dry season, early peoples could easily have connected them with the coming of the life-giving rains. The god Quetzalcoatl brought corn—Mesoamerica's most important crop—to the people. The quetzal itself is associated with corn, too: Its gracefully bending tail feathers are a traditional symbol for the green corn leaves.

*Stairway at the Temple of Quetzalcoatl in Teotihuacan.*

22

## THE EARLY GOD QUETZALCOATL

Quetzalcoatl changed over the course of Mesoamerican history. The ancient god Quetzalcoatl, the Plumed Serpent, was honored by peoples across Mesoamerica since before recorded history. He was originally a powerful creator god who participated in the recurring creation and destruction of the cosmos. He also brought the bones of the dead from the underworld, sprinkled them with his blood, and thus created the human race. He changed himself into a black ant, ventured into Sustenance Mountain, and brought back corn to feed the people.

## THE GOD AND THE MAN

During Toltec times, a priest of Quetzalcoatl took the name of the god for himself. This priest ruled the Toltec capital of Tula during the early years of its heyday. He is often called Topiltzin Quetzalcoatl (Our Young Prince the Plumed Serpent) to distinguish him from the original god. He is also called Ce Acatl Quetzalcoatl, for he was born in the year named Ce Acatl (One Reed) in the Toltec calendar.

Topiltzin Quetzalcoatl is a confusing historical figure, because different stories depict him in very different ways. Perhaps two priests of the Feathered Serpent, with the same name but differing attitudes, ruled at different times. An Aztec version of Topiltzin Quetzalcoatl's life says he was a warrior who fought alongside his father. After his father was killed in battle, Quetzalcoatl buried his body in Cloud Serpent Mountain, then captured his father's killers and sacrificed them on the mountain where his father's body rested.

In the other, more common and probably earlier version, Topiltzin Quetzalcoatl appears to have been a spiritual and benevolent ruler who encouraged people to offer flowers, snakes, birds, and butterflies to the Creator. Topiltzin Quetzalcoatl eventually lost out in a political battle with priests of darker forces who insisted on the importance of human sacrifice. He was exiled from Tula and fled eastward. When he reached the shores of the Gulf of Mexico, one ancient version of the story says, Quetzalcoatl set himself on fire. Then "the heart of Quetzalcoatl rose to heaven and, according to the elders, was transformed into the Morning Star…and Quetzalcoatl was called Lord of the Dawn." In this way, Quetzalcoatl became Venus, the morning star, which is an important symbol of renewal in Mesoamerica. The other version of Quetzalcoatl's fate recounts that he sailed away on a raft of serpents, promising to return at a time in the future when the year of his birth, Ce Acatl, came around again on the cyclical Mesoamerican calendar.

# THE AZTEC COLLAPSE

Later, the Aztecs idealized Topiltzin Quetzalcoatl and his era, when Toltec culture flourished. "Truly with him it began, truly from him it flowed out, from Quetzalcoatl—all art and knowledge," the Aztecs declared. The legend that he would return someday to reclaim his role as ruler became part of Aztec belief.

Aztec civilization dominated much of Mesoamerica for about one hundred and fifty years, until the arrival of the galleons of Hernando Cortés on the shores of the Gulf of Mexico in 1519. Despite their greater numbers, the Aztecs were completely conquered within two years. The legend of Quetzalcoatl and his promise to return may have had much to do with their rapid defeat.

Strange omens had been haunting the Aztecs for ten years before the white men came. A great temple had burst into flames and burned to the ground. Legend has it that a bird with a mirror on its chest was captured and taken to Moctezuma. When the great ruler looked into the mirror, he saw warriors riding on the backs of deer. So when his spies described winged towers that floated on the sea and bearded men with white skin riding strange deerlike animals (horses), Moctezuma and his wise men were concerned. Quetzalcoatl had prophesied he would return in the year Ce Acatl, which occurs once every fifty-two years in the Aztec calendar. That year was Ce Acatl—had Quetzalcoatl come back to reclaim his people?

Moctezuma sent a welcoming party to greet Cortés. They clothed the Spaniard in the sacred costume of Quetzalcoatl, "a turquoise mosaic snake mask with the head fan of quetzal feathers," according to Franciscan friar Bernardino de Sahagún, who worked in and around Tenochtitlan just after the fall of the Aztec empire. Arm bands with outspread quetzal feathers and crisscrossed bands of shells and gold were placed on him. He was given a shield decorated with gold and mother-of-pearl as well as chest decorations. All these ornaments were also decorated with quetzal feathers. Cortés did not know how precious these gifts were. He had been expecting plenty of gold. He asked the Aztecs, "Are these all your gifts of greeting, all your gifts for coming?"

After his messengers returned with news of the encounter with the Spaniards, Moctezuma was still unsure whether Cortés was truly Quetzalcoatl. The Aztec ruler invited Cortés and his soldiers into the royal palace as guests. Once inside, the Spanish took Moctezuma hostage. He allowed them to take over, probably because of his belief that Quetzalcoatl had returned. This gave the Spanish a critical advantage, and although the Aztecs eventually turned on them, the Spanish defeated the mighty empire relatively quickly.

24

*The meeting of Cortés and Moctezuma.*

## THE ANCIENT CULTURES CONTINUE

When the conquistadores conquered Mesoamerica, they imposed the Catholic faith on the people and tried to wipe out what they considered to be primitive beliefs and religious practices. But their success was only partial. Although Catholicism is the predominant religion in the area today, it has fused with ancient practices, creating a number of unique spiritual traditions and rituals.

In the mountainous states of Mexico, a striking example of this melding of traditions thrives during fiestas held on the feast day of a particular village's patron saint or during Holy Week (the week before Easter). Along with processions hon-

Quetzales *dancers reenact an ancient celebration in modern Mexico.*

oring Christ, the Virgin Mary, and the saints, ancient rituals honoring the spirits of the cosmos are also held. One is the *voladores*, a dance in which men dressed to represent sun-dedicated birds such as the eagle or macaw "fly" to the ground from a tall pole, to which they are attached by a rope. Another is the *quetzales*. The *quetzales* dancers wear huge, colorful fan-shaped headdresses atop cone-shaped hats. They are accompanied only by a flute, drum, and the rattles they carry in one hand. This dance is so ancient that only its name hints at its origin and meaning—that in the faded past, it almost certainly honored the mysterious quetzal bird itself.

*A male quetzal sits quietly on a branch.*

# FOUR

# LIFE OF THE QUETZAL

THE MALE QUETZAL PERCHES QUIETLY on a nearby tree branch, his bright red breast facing us. The sunbeams play on his iridescent green head and throat as he slowly turns his head, looking this way and that. His delicate, gleaming, flowing tail feathers sway gently in the breeze. Unlike many birds that jerk their heads nervously back and forth, he is calm and dignified. Both from his beauty and his demeanor it is easy to understand why the ancients held him to be sacred.

Suddenly he takes flight, quickly swooping downward to land on a nearby dead tree. He pauses a moment, then slips his body into a hole in the trunk. His graceful tail feathers drape down along the bark, the only clue to his presence inside the nest hole.

Tropical birds like the quetzal are adapted to a year with two seasons—rainy and dry. In Central America, the dry season begins in December and ends in April. Dry is a relative term, however—heavy rains may fall in the rain forests during any month, and the cloud forests in the highlands may also experience rain at any time. Even when it is not raining, the cloud forest is usually cloaked in a misty fog that coats every leaf with moisture.

## STARTING A FAMILY

Many mysteries remain about the behavior of this rare bird. It is known that the mating season of the quetzal begins just before the rainy season. Costa Rican research shows that at the end of the breeding season the male and female go their separate ways but reunite the following spring to raise a new family together in the territory they had inhabited before. The male courts the female with a looping flight up into the sky and back down again. Because each pair has its own individual territory, only one male displays in a specific area.

No one knows what brings about the male's more spectacular snakelike spiral followed by the plunge into the forest below. Perhaps the little-seen mass display of males occurs when a male has died and other males vie for the attention of his former mate.

The mated pair searches for a dead, decaying tree in which to hollow out a nest. The entrance hole to the nest is from fourteen to ninety feet (4.3 to 27 meters) above the ground. The nests are usually inside the forest, but sometimes they are at the edge of a pasture or even in a stump out in the open. After the pair has prepared a satisfactory nest and mated, the female lays two light blue eggs about an inch and a half (3.9 centimeters) long.

*Quetzal eggs in their tree-hole nest.*

The male and female birds take turns sitting on the eggs to keep them warm. Guatemalan natives used to claim that a quetzal nest had two entrance holes, for the convenience of the male bird. He could enter by one hole, his gorgeous feathers draped outside. Then, when he left, he could fly out the other hole, never having to turn around and damage his delicate tail. But in truth, a quetzal nest has only one hole, and the male bird often breaks off some or all of his long tail feathers during the breeding season as he takes his turns of duty at the nest.

*A male quetzal peeks out of the nest hole while incubating eggs.*

## RAISING THE CHICKS

After about eighteen days, the naked, pink chicks hatch. Their eyes are still glued shut, and they are completely helpless. Like all young birds they are hungry, and their parents are kept busy. While one parent sits on the nest, keeping the chicks warm, the other parent hunts for food, mostly small insects. By this time the rainy season is under way, and food is abundant. The chicks grow fast, and when they are eight days old, their eyes open.

At eight days, the chicks also have enough feathers to keep their bodies warm inside the protected nest cavity. Both parents can then gather food. Even so, one parent remains on guard much of the time. The eggs and chicks have a number of enemies, and broods are lost in two-thirds to three-quarters of the nests. The parents vigorously chase off squirrels that may eat the eggs. They also go after another tropical bird, called the emerald toucanet, that eats both the eggs and nestlings of other species. The short-tailed weasel, an expert predator, is most likely to succeed in getting a meal from a quetzal nest.

The male also keeps other quetzals out of the family's territory. He uses a soft, rhythmic whistle of paired notes to announce his claim. If a rival male comes near, giving out the same call, the territorial male will fly closer and challenge with his own whistle.

As they grow, the chicks are fed a varied diet—frogs, small lizards, land snails, and fruit, as well as insects. The chicks are soon covered with a motley coat of brown, buff, blackish, and green feathers. When they leave the nest, they are about

*It's hard to believe that chicks like this can grow up to be beautiful quetzals.*

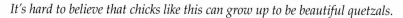

four weeks old. Unlike their parents, they have very short tail feathers, but they can fly short distances. The family stays together in the forest for a while as the parents continue to feed their chicks. But before long, the young birds are on their own.

A pair of quetzals may raise two broods of young each year, starting in March or early April and continuing until early August at the latest. But one brood each year is normal.

## QUETZALS THROUGHOUT THE YEAR

Even though quetzals feed on over forty different kinds of fruit, they specialize in the small fruits of more than a dozen species of wild avocado.

The rhythm of their lives is governed by the fruiting of these plants. They breed during the peak of avocado fruiting, when ten to fifteen different species have ripe fruit. And they are likely to leave the highlands when the avocados become scarce, even though other species of fruits are ripe and still available.

Throughout most of the year, the quetzals live quietly, scattered over the countryside. Despite their bright colors, quetzals blend in well with the tropical forest. The long plumes of the male can be mistaken for the fronds of ferns that grow attached to tree trunks, and the play of light and shadow across the birds' green backs melts into the overall greenness. The birds' slow movements also help make them inconspicuous. But when January comes again, the quetzals that left will return to the high cloud forests, showing off their breathtaking beauty and their versatile voices once more.

*Quetzal images are plentiful in modern Guatemalan textiles.*

# FIVE

# THE QUETZAL IN TODAY'S WORLD

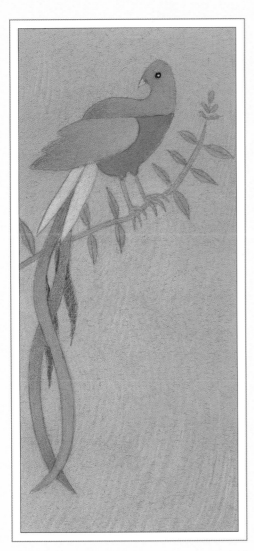

THE BOAT APPROACHES THE DOCK AT the Guatemalan village of Santiago Atitlán. We are eager to see what this tiny town has to offer visitors.

As we step ashore, children crowd around us, asking if we want to take their picture. Right by the dock is an open-air shop selling a variety of colorful rugs, blouses, and wall hangings. Along the front of the booth is a row of brightly colored cloth squares. Two male quetzals facing each other beak-to-beak occupy the center of each square, surrounded by concentric circles of triangles and flowers. Just up the street, white cloths embroidered with fanciful bright green quetzals are for sale. Another woman is offering a small square with an accurately represented quetzal in the center, surrounded by other birds of the region.

It is clear that the quetzal holds an important place in the imagination of this village. Quetzals once lived in the forests that used to cloak the sides of the nearby volcano, but the birds are absent now, along with most of the forest.

35

## THE QUETZAL AS A SYMBOL

In the marketplaces of Mayan villages throughout Guatemala, artisans sell a variety of quetzal images. In addition to embroidery incorporating likenesses of the bird, wooden masks often feature the dark face of a Mayan hero flanked by the image of a quetzal. Sometimes there is a quetzal on either side of his face. Rugs display a dark Mayan figure sitting cross-legged with hands raised on either side, each hand supporting a perched quetzal. This fellow may be a Mayan trader from the old days—the quetzal was a symbol of the merchants, and Quetzalcoatl was their patron.

*Quetzals decorate masks of ancient faces in Guatemalan marketplaces.*

Quetzal images appear throughout Guatemalan stories, as well as in the country's folk art. Perhaps the most compelling story involves the battle between the great Mayan chief Tecun Uman and the Spanish conqueror Pedro de Alvarado, which took place in 1523. During the battle, Alvarado's men slaughtered thirty thousand Mayans, including the brave chief, near what is now the city of Quetzaltenango. One version of the story says that when Tecun Uman fell, mortally wounded, quetzals fluttered down from the sky and settled on his breast, protecting his body from the cold throughout the night. When dawn came and the birds flew away, their once-white breasts had become stained red by the fallen hero's blood and remain red to this day.

The quetzal is the official bird of Guatemala, and the unit of Guatemalan currency is named after it. A magnificent flying male quetzal graces both the money and the Guatemalan flag. Mayan people in Guatemala today give a variety of answers when asked about the quetzal. "Yes," they say, "a quetzal cannot survive after it is captured. It will die of a broken heart. That is why it is the bird of freedom." Some believe that the bird's feathers will fall off if touched by a human hand, while others think of the quetzal as a symbol of death—if one flies through a house, a death will occur there soon.

## THE ENDANGERED QUETZAL

The quetzal may still thrive as a symbol, but its survival as a living bird is in great peril. Most of the cloud forests where it once lived have already been destroyed, and much of what forest remains is threatened by logging and farming. The large, ancient cloud-forest trees produce valuable lumber. Even in parks and preserves, loggers will cut down the trees if they can get away with it. As the human population of Mesoamerican countries continues to grow, more land is cleared for farms to raise corn and other crops, much of it for export.

Once, highland people in much of Mesoamerica shared their environment with quetzals, for the birds were a common sight in their natural surroundings. Today only those who can afford to travel to the few remote areas where quetzals still survive might be lucky enough to see them in the flesh.

Fortunately there is hope for this special bird. All six countries where the quetzal lives (Mexico, Guatemala, Honduras, El Salvador, Costa Rica, and Panama) have set aside parks where it is protected. But enforcement of protection costs money, a scarce commodity in developing countries. In addition, some of the parks are too small to support quetzal populations. The parks are also isolated from one another by deforested areas, making it difficult and dangerous for the birds to move from one area to another. The quetzal rarely survives captivity, and no one has ever succeeded in breeding captive birds, so saving the cloud forest is absolutely critical to this beautiful bird's existence.

However, quetzals need more than just the cloud forest for survival. Quetzals protected in the well-patrolled Monteverde Cloud Forest Preserve in Costa Rica leave and fly to lower elevations to feed at the end of the breeding season. Once the quetzals leave preserves, they are vulnerable to illegal killing for their beautiful feathers. In some areas, people kill quetzals for food. In addition, so much of the lower-elevation land in Central America has been turned into farms that the birds that leave the highlands can have trouble finding enough to eat during much of the year.

To protect quetzals from extinction, we must learn more about where they go after leaving protected areas. We need to find ways of assuring their safety and food supplies during the entire year, not only during the breeding season. Only then can we hope that this unique living symbol will continue to survive.

*A quetzal flies over a protected preserve, where it can live wild and free.*

# FURTHER READING

**Magazine Articles**

Bowes, Anne LaBastille. "The Quetzal, Fabulous Bird of Maya Land." *National Geographic* (January 1969): 141–50. Describes adventures in attempting to study quetzals during the 1960s.

Jukofsky, Diane. "Mystical Messenger." *Nature Conservancy* (November/December 1993): 24–27. About George Powell's research on quetzals in Guatemala.

McDowell, Bart. "The Aztecs." *National Geographic* (December 1980): 704–52. This article, full of color images, is followed by two others about the Aztecs.

**Books**

Berdan, Frances F. *The Aztecs.* Indians of North America Series. New York: Chelsea House, 1989. This paperback, with many illustrations, clearly discusses Aztec life.

Bierhorst, John. *The Mythology of Mexico and Central America.* New York: William Morrow, 1990. This book has few illustrations but covers the beliefs of Mesoamerican groups, including the Maya and Aztecs.

Coe, Michael D. *The Maya.* Fifth edition. New York: Thames and Hudson, 1993. Written by one of the world's experts on the subject, this book (available in paperback) thoroughly deals with Mayan history and culture.

Coe, Michael D. *Mexico: From the Olmecs to the Aztecs.* Fourth edition. New York: Thames and Hudson, 1994. Discusses the Maya and Aztecs as well as other, less-known groups that inhabited Mexico before the Conquest.

Day, Jane S. *Aztec: The World of Moctezuma.* Niwot, CO: Roberts Rinehart, 1992. This paperback was written in conjunction with an exhibition of Aztec artifacts at the Denver Museum of Natural History.

Garza, Mercedes de la. *The Mayas: 3,000 Years of Civilization.* Mexico City: Monclem Ediciones, 1992. This colorful book focuses mainly on Mayan art and architecture.

Janson, Thor. *Quetzal.* Guatemala City: Editorial Artemis Edinter, 1992. This book, by a man who has studied quetzals for more than ten years, is hard to find but worth looking for. It features many beautiful full-color photographs, as well as valuable information.

Stuart, Gene S., and George E. Stuart. *Lost Kingdoms of the Maya.* Washington, D.C.: National Geographic Society, 1993. This beautiful book focuses on Mayan life in times both ancient and modern.

# INDEX

Illustrations are in **boldface.**